WHAT DOES LOVE LOOK LIKE?

JANETTE OKE

illustrated by CHERI BLADHOLM

BETHANY BACKYARD®

www.bethanyhouse.com

WHAT DOES

LOOK LIKE?

Design and production: Lookout Design Group, Inc.

Printed in China.

Library of Congress Cataloging-in-Publication Data applied for

Dedicated with welcoming love to expected
grandchild number eleven—firstborn of Lavon
and Monica Oke. You are in our prayers.

—JANETTE OKE

A special thanks to Mrs. Joanne Cole and her first-
grade class at Faith Heritage School in Syracuse,
New York, for modeling for this book.

—CHERI BLADHOLM

Hesitantly, Emily stepped into the classroom—her new classroom. The room was already full of children, and she suddenly felt shy and alone.

Too quickly, though, the teacher turned to her. "Welcome, Emily. We've been expecting you. I'm Mrs. Crayton." Emily liked her smile. "Class, this is Emily Walters. We have all worn name tags today—just for you." Mrs. Crayton reached out a hand and led Emily to a desk near the back of the room. "We hope you'll enjoy our classroom."

Emily slid into the chair, not daring to look around. Perhaps if she was very quiet, they would all forget about the new girl in the back row.

Mrs. Crayton removed her reading glasses and set them on her desk. "We have been learning all about things you can see and measure this week. But there are many things that you can't hold in your hand or touch. Things you can't measure with a ruler or in ounces. And they are just as real."

A boy in the first row shuffled his feet. "You mean, like air?"

"That's a very good observation, Bobby, but air can be measured."

One girl near Emily giggled, and Emily felt badly for Bobby. What if she had said the same thing?

"You and I can't measure air," went on Mrs. Crayton. "I can't say to you, 'Give me a cupful of air. Or pour a little more air into my pail.' But there are instruments that can measure air, so we know a lot about it." Mrs. Crayton paused for a moment. "I was thinking of totally different things. Like love, for instance. Is love real?"

Several heads nodded energetically. A few of Emily's classmates even dared to say "yes" all in chorus, soft and drawn out.

"But, if you were to draw a picture of love, what would you draw?"

A girl with brown pigtails raised her hand and waved it about like a little flag, her eyes sparkling. "Can we draw it?" she asked.

The whole class groaned, except for Emily.

One boy spoke up, frustration edging his voice. "Teacher just said that you can't draw it," he corrected.

"Maybe you can," broke in Mrs. Crayton. "Maybe we can't draw love like we would draw a bird or a tree. But it might be fun to draw ideas. I think that's a wonderful plan, Liz."

Another groan.

A smile lit Mrs. Crayton's face. "Let's use our imaginations and think. Let's draw some pictures that help us to understand—to define what love is. Now, I know there are people who show you love in many different ways, so let's think about that feeling and how love might look if you could draw it."

Emily frowned as she carefully took out a sheet of paper and her new box of crayons. It was hard enough to draw rabbits or cats. But love—who could draw that?

8

The sixteen students leaned over desks, drawing and erasing. Crayons scratched against paper, and chairs scraped against the floor as bodies shifted. Everyone was busy making a picture of love.

Without warning, Emily's green crayon snapped, one half falling to the floor. Embarrassed, she helplessly watched as it rolled under her neighbor's desk.

The other girl saw it. She reached down, her blue eyes twinkling. Emily noticed her nametag. *Krista.* Krista handed the broken crayon back to Emily.

Emily smiled shyly as she took the broken crayon. She wondered if she dared whisper thanks.

After several more minutes, Mrs. Crayton stood. "I think it's time to see where your imaginations have taken you," she announced. "Who would like to be first?"

Emily slid low in her chair, hoping no one would volunteer her.

She was thankful when Stacy raised her hand. Stacy scrambled from her desk and marched to the front of the class, where she held her picture up high.

"Tell us why you drew a flower, Stacy," prompted the teacher.

"I think love would be pretty and have bright colors. It makes people feel happy inside." Stacy beamed—first toward Mrs. Crayton, then toward the entire class.

"Very good," said Mrs. Crayton, and the class clapped.

13

14

The next girl held up a white piece of paper with two people. One held a big chocolate bar that she had broken in two and was handing one piece to the other person. Emily thought it was a nice picture.

"Let's see what you have to share, Barkley."

Barkley walked up, waving his yellow sheet.
In the middle was a bold, brown square. "I think
love is like a big, big blanket—big enough to
wrap up the whole world. All warm like my
grandma Smith's goosedown."

He grinned and swung into his seat.

And then it was the girl next to Emily's turn. "This is a tree," Krista began, wriggling nervously.

Someone smothered a laugh at a stern look from Mrs. Clayton.

Krista wriggled even more and turned back to her picture, not looking at her classmates. "I think . . . I think that love has lots of branches. The branches are people. Each person has a tree, and it grows and grows, bigger and bigger, the more people you love."

Krista's idea had been a good one. Emily glanced down at her own sheet, suddenly unsure.

Down the row they went. One girl had kind of a messy sheet. "I think love is like a big, long, humongous table, with a place for everyone."

The next boy to stomp up held his picture in one hand, high over his head. "It's like a big, round globe," he explained. "Everyone in the whole wide world is in it."

Mrs. Crayton nodded. "I hear many of you saying that love is for everyone," she said, "and that is good. Very good."

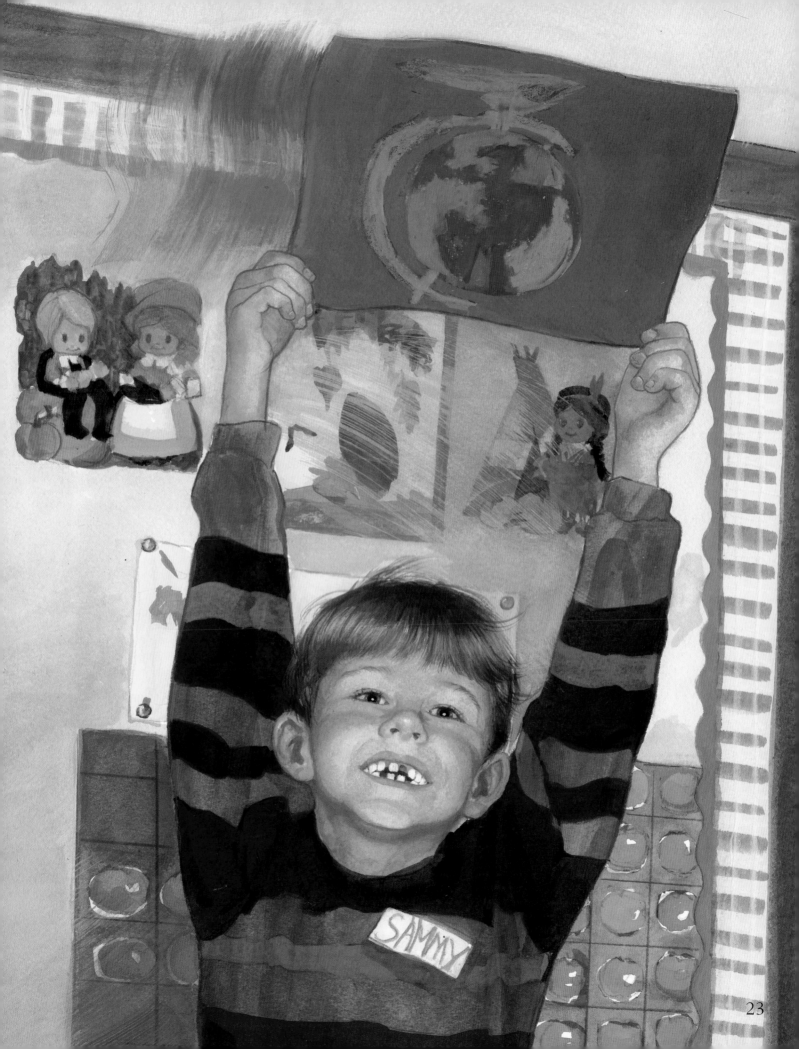

A girl thumped to the front of the room on her crutches, her paper scrunched against the hard wood. She stopped and tried to rub out the creases with her palm before turning the orange paper to the class. "In a circle, there are no rough edges to hurt people. And no corners for anyone to get pushed in—and not noticed. The circle can get larger and larger to let more people in."

On they went down the rows. Emily found the
nervous tingle in her tummy leaving as she heard
about happy faces, umbrellas, bright yellow suns,
fuzzy slippers, and a warm fireplace. There were
so many good ideas about love!

And then Mrs. Crayton was
saying softly, "And now it is our
new student's turn. Emily, do
you have a picture for us?"

Emily rose slowly from her seat and dipped her head shyly. She picked up her sheet of light blue paper—her favorite color—and walked to the front of the room. She didn't feel quite as new now, nor quite as scared, but she still felt a bit unsure about showing her picture to the whole class.

She took a deep breath as she held it up. "I think this is how love looks," she said. To her surprise, her voice sounded loud enough for the entire class to hear.

For a long moment, the room was silent. A few of Emily's classmates wrinkled their foreheads in confusion, and others whispered to each other. Some nodded their heads, and three or four even smiled.

The silence was broken by the loud sound of Mrs. Crayton clapping. Others joined in, until soon everyone was applauding.

"I think we should put Emily's picture on the special merit board," suggested Stacy.

With a nod and a smile, Mrs. Crayton took out some tape and handed it to Emily.

No one rushed from the classroom when the recess buzzer sounded. They all sat and watched as Emily walked to the special merit board and hung her picture up high, where everyone could see it.

EPILOGUE

You can read all about this great love in the Bible—God's Word. In the book of John it tells us that God loved the world so much that He sent His only Son, Jesus, to die in our place, paying the penalty for the sins that have separated us from a loving God. We are to accept this love and God's pardon, feel sorry for our wrongdoing, and ask Him to give us a new, clean heart so that we can be welcomed into the wonderful place called Heaven when we die.

Read the book of John. It will tell you the whole, amazing story—a story all about LOVE.

Janette's granddaughter Emily and the picture that inspired this book.